I0738895

Teardrops of Blood

Other Books by Marlo Donald

Crying From the Pain

Available on

www.MarloDonald.com

And wherever books are sold

Teardrops of Blood

Marlo Donald

Word in Due Season Publishing, LLC

Teardrops of Blood

Marlo Donald

Word in Due Season Publishing, LLC
P.O. Box 210013
Auburn Hills, Michigan 48321-0921

Cover Design by Cover Me Book Covers

ISBN 13: 978-0-9829686-7-3
Library of Congress Control Number: 2018903539

Disclaimer

This is a work of fiction. Names, characters, businesses, places, events, locales, and incidents are either the products of the author's imagination or used in a fictitious manner. Any resemblance to actual persons, living or dead, or actual events is purely coincidental.

I dedicate this book to The Trinity:

God, Jesus and the Holy Spirit.

Thank You for everything You have done for me.

And to my children and grandchildren.

I love you.

Never lose hope,

The Trinity will prevail.

Prologue

It was a beautiful day, yet my insides felt dark and gloomy as I prepared my clothes to go to work at Chabo the next day. I felt like I was dying; I cried a lot the day before until I made myself stop. Suddenly, I burst into tears again and I didn't know why. I cried all day. I was a strong individual. I don't cry. I knew something was wrong; therefore, I went to emergency care.

I explained to the doctor how I had been crying for two days and I didn't know what was going on. All I do is go to work and back home. I told him about the distressing situation I was in at the job. His look of concern confirmed at that very moment he knew, and I knew "they" were the reason for all the tears.

All the years of harassment and arguing had hunted me down. I didn't like the feeling. It hurt. What was the heaviness that resided in my mind, my heart, my life, that caused an unending flow of tears? I never felt this before, but that day I was introduced to it.

The doctor said, "Asia, what you're dealing with has a name…it's depression."

This is how I got there.

Chapter 1

I am a young lady who was trying to navigate her way through life and take care of her children. I'm an intelligent woman who had dreams of becoming a fashion designer. However, I didn't quite know how to pursue that dream. I was involved in an unstable relationship while fighting off demons from my childhood. My mate at the time thought drug dealing was the only way of survival and I had no desire to continue with that lifestyle. Although living "hood rich" was nice, it wasn't the life I wanted. I loved having money; but wanted it the honest way. No more looking over my shoulders wondering when the police would come rushing in my home again. No more ducking and dodging. If he didn't want to work, that was on him. I needed to work.

I had no one who could take me to work when I started my first job. I rode a bike, caught the bus, did whatever I had to do to get there. My mate and I worked at the same job, however I needed my space at work. Therefore, I quit the job. I didn't know what was next, but I decided to step out on faith.

I put in applications everywhere I could think of. I landed a temporary job at Chabo that turned into a permanent job. It had a decent pay rate with full health benefits, retirement package and a 401(k) plan. It was enough for me and my kids to survive; but it came with a hefty price that almost cost me everything I had, including my sanity.

Chapter 2

I received a phone call from a temporary agency, asking me if I wanted to work at Chabo for a couple of weeks planting some flowers, which I accepted. It was something to do to make a couple of extra dollars. I had no intention of it being a long-term position. But that's what it turned into.

Chabo was a government agency. The department I went to took care of various outdoor tasks throughout the city. I worked with a different person each day. It was a male-dominated place with one woman before I got there. After I arrived, a Hispanic woman came. Then a couple weeks later, two Caucasian women came. I was the only African-American woman.

At first glance, it seemed to be a fun place to work. I never engaged with Caucasians before; I was looking forward to the new experiences. The first couple of weeks were fine with virtually no problems. But that didn't last for long. About a month later, I started to see and hear things I had never experienced before.

Liam was a boss; he was a short, thin man with blonde hair. He and some of the others were going out for drinks. Tammy, a coworker, with a medium build and brunette hair, asked me if I would like to join them. I later found out she had a reputation for sleeping around with Liam and some of the other coworkers. In my effort to try to fit in and build a relationship with them, I went also.

The bar was a cold, dark room filled with cigarette smoke. You could see people doing illegal drug activities in the corner. Some were drunk, loud, and having what they thought was a good time. I stuck out because I was the only black person in the room, but I didn't care. I was trying to enjoy my coworkers. After a while, we were drunk. As I was sitting there, Liam and I began to talk.

He looked at me and said, "I don't like black people. A black person killed one of my relatives."

I looked at him in total disbelief. *I can't believe he just opened his mouth and said that to me. Doesn't he see I am black?* I walked away feeling ashamed and totally misunderstood. I pulled Tammy to the side and told her what just happened. I started crying. I was hurt and confused. I just had my first major encounter with racism.

When I got to work the next day, Liam called me in the office. He looked at me and said, "I never said I didn't like you." He grabbed me and tried to kiss me. Shocked, I pulled away from him. Everything seemed to go quiet. The air was so crisp you could hear a pin drop. My mind went back to the moment I was raped as a teenager. I was nervous and scared. I knew I had to get away from him. *I don't want to be raped again.*

I ran out of the room as fast as I could. Zac, a coworker and a union steward, was the first person I encountered as I was heading out.

He looked at me and asked, "What's wrong?"

I told him what happened.

He said, "Well, there's nothing you can do about it because you have no witnesses. It's your word against his."

After I didn't accept Liam's advancements, he resented me. He had power and he was going to use it to do everything he could to either make me miserable or make me quit. He started giving me the hardest and the dirtiest jobs. He tried to get under my skin, but it didn't faze me because I was not scared of hard work or getting dirty. He didn't know I used to be a tomboy.

Chapter 3

I started hanging out with Tammy after work since we both liked to party. But, I didn't know she was telling everything we were doing. Her drugs of choice were alcohol with cocaine; mine were alcohol with marijuana, which was not a problem for me on the job at the time because I didn't have a commercial driver's license (CDL). Those who carried a CDL were the only ones who got drug tested. When Tammy got tested, Liam was her look-out guy. He always warned her when it was testing time or if she would be one of the supposed random picks to get tested. She was always able to escape.

As time went by, I worked various jobs that required me to get a CDL, which opened an avenue for Liam and his boss, Darryl, to drug test me. Darryl was a small guy with an enormous ego. He ran multiple departments and the boss of our bosses. Darryl would turn his nose up and roll his eyes every time he saw me. I was still a temporary employee at this point, so I didn't care. I wasn't planning on sticking around with those ignorant people anyway. I was just using it for what it was worth: a paycheck.

Temporary employees worked nine months and got laid off for three months. The end of my nine months was approaching. They were hiring for full time employment as I approached my ninth month. I filled out an application, with no expectation of being hired. It was worth a shot. Right before my three-month layoff, I got busted on a drug test for marijuana. When I left for the layoff, they didn't call me back. Others flunked the drug test and they were still working. However, Chabo used this as an opportunity to get rid of me. I wrote Darryl's boss a letter, telling her about all the drinking and cocaine usage I'd witnessed while working at Chabo. I wasn't expecting anything to come from it, I only wanted to inform her I found enjoyable, peaceful employment elsewhere.

Chapter 4

About two months later, Darryl called me. I was shocked. *What does he want?*

"How are you doing?" Daryl asked.

"Fine."

"Are you working?"

"Yes, I am."

He said, "Well, I want you to come back."

"I'm not coming back as a temporary employee."

"No, you won't be a temp. You're hired as a full-time employee. You can start next week."

"I'll be there!"

I was surprised. They were offering me a full-time job when I knew they didn't like me and wouldn't even return my phone calls. *What happened?* I accepted the offer because it was good pay with full benefits, and I needed it.

***

When I got there, Reed, who was one of my co-workers, told me Darryl's boss told him that he'd better find me and give me a job. Reed loved to keep up drama. At that time, Reed didn't work in our department, but he kept up with everything that was going on. Darryl and Liam were using him outside of work to handle things they needed done at their homes. The grin on Reed's face said he loved every minute of the situation.

Darryl didn't want to give me a job. The letter I wrote to his boss played a major role in his decision because of affirmative action, and because I am a black woman, a double minority. I could've sued the company for discrimination because they hired two Caucasian women and a Hispanic woman. To not hire a black employee wasn't a good look.

Darryl's boss was a Black woman. I didn't know at the time she was dealing with racial problems in her own department. Within a year of her making Daryl rehire me, she quit and went to work in a different state.

Liam backed off me for a while, He had others to holler at like he was the daddy and we were his children. He had a bad habit of fronting people off, especially over the radio where he was heard over the entire workplace. He started giving me a lot of jobs cutting grass or trimming trees. Over time, those jobs affected my health, making my physically ill. My face broke out, my eyes reddened.

One day, I was doing lawn mower maintenance in the equipment room. While we were working on equipment, Liam came in, looked at me and said, "You're ugly. Look at all those bumps in your face."

Everybody started laughing. I was so devastated, I couldn't respond. I tried to block out the laughter. I was mad, but I wasn't going to show it. I couldn't allow him to upset me. Although he left laughing, he appeared shaken by my response. Any other time, it would have turned into a full-blown argument. Bumping heads with him became normal for me. When I got to work, I waited on it. I knew it was only a matter of time before he was at it again. I argued with him more than I argued with my man. Liam was getting on my nerves.

He never tried anything sexual towards me again. His boss buddy, Darryl, started up. One day as I was walking up the ramp towards the lunch room, he looked at me and said, "Liam likes hips and butts."

"What are you telling me for? He isn't getting none of mine." I looked at him, rolled my eyes, and walked away.

Other incidents occurred with Darryl saying inappropriate things to me. One morning, I received my job assignment and was heading out. He looked at me and said, "My wife couldn't get me off last night." *What did he just say to me? I don't care; I'm not getting him off either.* I was pissed off, but I just walked away. Some of the other coworkers told me I should turn him in for sexual harassment. He would say inappropriate things right in front of them and made no effort to hide it. He didn't care who heard him. He was the overseer and he felt like he could say and do whatever he wanted.

I was scared. I didn't know how to fight this kind of fight. I was used to fighting physically, but I couldn't do that in this situation. I couldn't grab my baseball bat out of my car trunk and knock him upside his head like I would have done somebody from the streets who would've disrespected me like that. I couldn't call my family and say, "Come on right now, it's going down." I had to learn a new strategy and I had to learn it fast.

My name kept getting pulled for drug testing by this supposedly random name-picking system. I was going at least every three months. Some hadn't been in a couple of years. It was not a coincidence; they were trying to catch me dirty again. I couldn't go out like that, so I found ways to prevent getting caught.

They were pissed off because they knew I still smoked marijuana. Some of the coworkers knew people I knew outside of work. They were telling on me, but the company couldn't prove it, which made them resent me more. I did my job, I did it well, so that was one thing they couldn't complain about. Whether they liked me or not, I did what I was supposed to do.

Chapter 5

Some years later, it was finally time for Darryl to retire. I was so glad to get rid of him. *Whoever was taking his place couldn't be any worse than him.* His replacement's name was Barnes. Barnes was short with black hair. He had a cold-hearted stare that said "prejudice" when he looked at minorities. But, I didn't care. I wasn't kissing his butt just like I didn't kiss anybody else's.

Liam got some help; a new boss named Graham. The first time I saw him, he and Liam were walking down the hallway toward the lunchroom as I was leaving out of the lunch room. He looked at me, and I looked at him. He rolled his eyes so hard at me. The moment was cold and awkward. By this time, I had developed an I-don't-care attitude. If you step on my toes, I'm stepping back.

Graham had an olive complexion with long blonde hair. He had a medium build, tall and bow-legged. I heard from a secretary that he was nice when he worked in his former department. Graham started stirring up trouble for me right off the bat, always telling Liam I was doing this or that. One day, he told Liam I was on my cell phone while I was working. To my surprise, Liam asked him if I was doing my job while I was on the phone. He told him I was talking and working. Liam responded, "Well what do you want me to do about it? She was working." *Where did that come from? He didn't try to use it against me.* I was baffled. Graham continued his tricks, but most of them didn't work. He started acting aggressive. *Something was different about him.*

One day, as I was walking up the ramp heading to the rest room, I caught this guy handing Liam a white powdery substance in a flat square package. *I'm not dumb, that's cocaine he's buying.* That would explain the mood changes.

The next week, Liam and Graham both gave me a tough time. I guess they were mad because I saw the transaction, or they were just being themselves, nasty as usual. They sent me and Tammy to cut grass and weed whack about a ten block stretch with push mowers which would take us all week when a riding mower could have done most of it in a few hours.

It was extremely hot that day. I went to the lawn mower room and caught one of the guys on a riding mower. I asked him if he could do some of it for us. He did what he could before he was caught and got into trouble. We proceeded to do the rest. The next day, we were at it again. It was so hot I started feeling sick. I was dizzy and vomiting, but I didn't know why.

I wanted to go home, but I was due to leave early that day because I had a doctor's appointment. I knew if I told them, they would assume I was just trying to get out of that job assignment. They already gave me hell all week. I was afraid to sit down. If one of them came by and saw me, they would've said I was wasting time. So, I kept working through dizziness, nausea and vomiting.

It had to be the grace of God that allowed me to keep working through sickness because I don't know how I did it. When I got to the doctor, he said I was having a heat stroke and took me off work for a week. I went back to the job after my appointment. All the bosses were gone so I gave my doctor's excuse to the secretary and asked her to put a copy on the boss' desk, so they would know what was going on.

The next morning, Graham called asking me why I wasn't there before telling me that I would get written up as a "no-call no-show." I told him to see the secretary because I brought my excuse in. Disappointment filled his voice; he was mad and wanted to write me up because I wasn't there to finish that job assignment.

I don't know what I did to make him dislike me. I couldn't change the color of my skin or the fact that I'm a woman. I'm also not the kind of woman that would have sex with whomever. I wasn't about to change just to keep a job. When I returned to work, they were mad because I had a week off as if I was on vacation. The first thing they did was send me to get drug tested. I didn't care. I was prepared for it.

As time went on, I started feeling sick all the time. Hay fever, sinus infections, irritated eyes, no energy, equilibrium imbalance. My doctor couldn't fix it and I didn't know what I was going to do.

As I was sitting in the clinic waiting to be drug tested, I was looking through a magazine and saw an ad describing the symptoms I was experiencing. It said you may be allergic to something and you should go see this allergy doctor. I called and made an appointment.

When I went to see the allergist, he said he saw signs of depression. I ignored it. *Whatever, I'm okay.* The test showed I was allergic to all pollen, all grass and all trees. That's why I was sick. I worked with pollen every day. He started giving me injections that was made of everything I was allergic to. It was supposed to make me become immune to it. The injections didn't work right away. I was still sick. He took me off work for three months to get my system adjusted properly to the injections.

While I was off, Chabo employees would ride by my house and follow me everywhere, trying to see what I was doing. Tammy would call me and tell me that Liam said he seen me here or there. *I had to take care of my business.* They thought I was lying about being sick. I guess they thought I paid the doctor to say and do the things he did. *These are the most dysfunctional people I ever seen in my life. I've run across some characters, but none like this.* They were like the "good ole boys." If you're one of us, you're fine. But if you're not, you're considered an enemy and a threat, especially when you don't play by their rules.

Chapter 6

Three months passed, and I was feeling a little better, although not completely healed. They didn't pay me my sick leave pay, so I had to file a grievance. Barnes told me in the grievance meeting that I should quit the job if I couldn't do it. *Are you stupid? I knew others who had medical issues that they worked around. You're going to work around mine, too.*

They were aware the doctor told me to stay away from chipping brush or cutting trees because that produced a lot of saw dust. But it went in one ear and out of the other one. When they wanted to be ignorant, they would put me on those types of jobs, then be mad when I called in sick.

A lot of employees bent over backwards trying to stay in their grace. They were backstabbing each other and whatever else they could do to try to get promoted or keep their jobs, like this guy named Harnes. He had one of the lowest positions out of what was considered as one of the lowest departments. Suddenly, he became a foreman in our department although he was unqualified. Harnes was a black man with a light complexion and long hair. He looked like he was mixed. The first time they sent him out to salt the roads, he went a half of a block and dumped his entire load of salt on the ground. They had to take the bucket loader and scrape it up. *But this is who y'all made a foreman? What a joke.*

Tammy loved him. She thought he was one of the nicest looking guys at the job. She said she was going to get him. That didn't happen. There was a young lady who Darryl and Liam brought in with the promise of giving her a full-time job. They had other intentions for her that were not work-related. There were no plans to giving her a full-time job. That was just one of their broken promises to get her to do what they wanted her to do: sexual favors.

They met her at one of those restaurants where the girls wear tight, skimpy clothes. They thought she would be easy prey. She was, but not with them. She hooked up with Harnes. They got caught having sex in the secretary's stock room. They hit it off so well, she got pregnant and they got married. Harnes wasn't faithful. She was wife number six, so she should have known better. It was rumored that he was having multiple affairs. They eventually let her go from the job. He had free range to sleep around with anyone who was willing on the job.

Chapter 7

A few years later, Liam got busted on a drug test. He used to come to work drunk all the time. I couldn't believe they let it go that far. It had been so much with this guy for so many years, Darryl's boss, the head administrator, gave him the option to get fired or retire. He chose to leave so he wouldn't lose his pension. I was so happy he was leaving. *Things have got to get better now since Darryl and Liam are gone.* I had never been more wrong in my life.

Graham was the head foreman and his drug use had him out of control. Harnes and their boss Barnes didn't know how to run the department. Things went downhill really fast. Harry had been trying for years to get his say-so on what was going on in our department. There was less dirty work and a lot of overtime involved compared to his department. Harry thought he was the toughest person around. I heard about him through various people he had problems with. He was a head foreman in a department outside of our sector. He and Liam used to bump heads a lot because he would try to run his department and ours, too. He ran his crew like they were army recruits and he was the sergeant.

Liam wasn't having any of that. He knew if this guy got his say-so in this department, it would be trouble for them. Liam was gone now; Graham or Harnes couldn't stand up against him. Harry saw this as his opportunity to finally get his way in our department. The effect of Harry's way of doing things didn't show up right away; but it crept in slowly.

Our department started making some vehicle changes; they were adding more trucks with airbrakes. A lot of us didn't have an Air Brake endorsement because it wasn't needed. The changing of the vehicles that were equipped with air brakes forced us to get the endorsement. It wasn't an urgency for me because the first batch of vehicles they got with air brakes were for dealing with trees, which I was allergic to. I didn't know they would eventually use that to their advantage to screw me over.

Tammy had a hard time passing the test because she never took the first CDL test because she was grandfathered in. Things had changed. Her buddy Liam was gone, so she had no one to pull strings for her anymore. She was going to have to work it out on her own.

When I got to work the next morning, Tammy told me

she had a meeting with Barnes about her Air Brake endorsement. It was break time, so I went upstairs to use the restroom. When I got in there, it was peaceful. I enjoyed those few moments of alone time. Our bathroom stayed clean and there weren't many women there to mess it up. I was standing by the shower area when Tammy rushed in shaking. She looked nervous and scared.

"What's wrong with you?" I asked.

"Nothing," she replied, almost in tears.

I noticed the creamy substance on her face, which I inquired about. She said she busted a pimple while wiping the creamy substance off her face. I knew that was a lie. If that had been a pimple, when she wiped it away it would have still been oozing puss. It didn't. I think Barnes had her give him oral sex in exchange for preventing her layoff. The thought of it made me sick to my stomach. I can't believe she did that to him. They were out of control and she needed to stop.

A couple of weeks later, I got to work, and everybody was talking about how Tammy got laid off. *What? After she gave him oral sex and whatever else she did, they still laid her off?* These people are animals. She should have known better. It took a month for her to pass the written part of the driver's license test. She came back to work, looking ashamed.

Chapter 8

Graham was so comfortable with his drug use on the job, one day as he gave out job orders, he had snorted so much cocaine that it was falling out of his nose. I called the chief union steward, Cody, and told him what was going on. I later found out Cody was only pretending to do his job. He really didn't care about us. They were paying him off not to help us. He said he was about to make some phone calls to some higher-ups to tell them he needed to get drug tested. *They're running me in every couple of months and I don't get high at work.*

Cody called me back, like I already knew they didn't do anything to Graham. He was a foreman, so he could do whatever he wanted to do whenever he wanted to do it. They thought they were protecting Graham, but they were actually hurting him. He thought he was untouchable. He kept coming to work under the influence; the higher ups didn't seem to care.

A month or so later, when I got to work, everybody was laughing and carrying on. They showed me a newspaper article that stated Graham was so high, he knocked down a few of his neighbor's fences, tore up some lawns and cars. The neighbors had to call the police to make him stop. He went to jail but tried to say he was high from prescription medications. He had a lot of friends in the judicial system he always bragged about. He only got a slap on the wrist. He didn't have to be on probation or nothing else. *Wow! If that would've been me, I would be in jail and I would've been fired, too. But not him. He was in the good ole boys club. They had benefits.* He was pissed off because he knew everybody knew and they teased him about it. He was doing everything in his power to make me miserable. I was getting fed up with him.

A friend of mine asked my boyfriend and I if we would like to go up north to go fishing with them when I got off work. I needed to get away. I was stressed from all the fussing and fighting at work, plus from a stressful relationship at home.

We packed up and headed out. We were almost there when that little voice inside of me, the Holy Spirit, kept tugging at me telling me to go back home. I knew something was wrong, so I told my friend's boyfriend to please take us back home. He didn't want to. He was mad because we had just arrived at our destination.

"I don't care; I got to go home. I don't know why but I do." The mood in the truck was quiet and tense. He was mad at me, but I didn't care. When I got home, there was a note on my door from Child Protective Services. *What does Child Protective Services want with me?* I called them. They said my cousin who was in my care told them she had been sexually molested by a friend of the family. My heart dropped to the bottom of my shoe. They told me to go to the school because that's where she made the allegations.

I took the next day off work to go to the school. The security guard plus a few others told me what took place. The school was noisy. Kids were out of control running everywhere. The principal was snooty with her pride high as the clouds. The security guard looked like she was in disbelief. It was a chaotic scene, an unpleasant situation to be in.

I found out my cousin told everyone in the school, all the students including the staff. Everyone knew but me. I went through the protocol to get the situation resolved. Child Protective Services, for whatever reason, said she wasn't telling the truth. A lot of my coworkers' kids went to the same school. So, the allegations followed me to work. *This is one of the most hurtful, embarrassing situations I'd ever been in.*

People on the job were whispering and laughing about it like it was a joke. Meanwhile, a piece of me was dying inside. While Graham was giving out job assignments, he looked at me and said, "At least nobody's molesting my kids." *What the hell did he just say?* I wanted to jump over the table to beat him. I was pissed. This was the last straw.

I already had it in my mind that he had one more time and this thing was going to get physical. This was it! I didn't care about losing my job, going to jail or anything else at this point. I'm whooping his behind. When I got off work, that's all I could think about. *It's going down; he done crossed the line.* It plagued my mind all day and night.

I got up to get ready for work. *Lord, take care of my kids, help me get out of jail. I'm whooping him today.* I was ready. I was prepared for whatever price I had to pay. I didn't care; I wanted revenge. At that moment, Joyce Meyers came on. I watched her show every morning before I went to work. I don't know why, but I did. I wasn't trying to live a holy life, although I had a relationship with the

Lord. I talked to Him on a regular basis when I was high, drunk or sober. I always kept it real with Him. He knew whatever condition I was in when I was in it, so I never tried to hide anything from him. I was listening and not listening because I was trying to get ready when she started talking about unruly bosses, how we should treat them, and why they may be acting the way they are acting. She was hitting on a few subjects I was dealing with at that moment. I sat down.

"Lord, are you talking to me?"

He said, "Yes."

At that moment, I felt a calm come over me. Peace entered my mind. His presence entered the room. He told me to calm down, everything was going to be okay. You just sit back. Be patient. This battle is Mine, not yours. I've been using you.

I stepped back and took a deep breath, laughed, thought to myself, *God just saved you from some serious injury, Graham*. He also saved me from some legal trouble. When I got to work, he was handing out job orders. He looked at me as if he was mad because I wasn't mad. I was still hurt and embarrassed, but I wasn't going to give him the pleasure of knowing it. He tried his best to get me upset. Graham gave me a job to go chip brush, trying to make me get sick again. *I didn't care because when I'm not feeling good, I will call in sick, stay home, and take care of myself.*

Chapter 9

Over time a lot of the original coworkers were leaving, some retiring others on disability. Harnes brought in his friends from his old department. Their old department was shut down. His friends who didn't have enough seniority got laid off. They filled the empty positions in our department with them. They came in kissing Harnes' behind. They did work for him at his home and worked on his cars in their attempt to gain a higher position to protect themselves from layoff. If you had a higher position than a person with more seniority, the person with the seniority would get laid off first because their position was lower.

With most people gone, Zach went up in status because he knew how to do all the jobs and operate all the equipment. *He was a good worker.* He asked to work with me a lot because he knew I would get the job done. What I didn't know at the time was that he went around lying, telling people we were sleeping with each other. When we were on third shift, we would hide out and catch a nod on break time. That's the only "sleeping together" we did.

He would always say some slick stuff in a joking way, but never said or did anything straight forward that made me uncomfortable. We used to go to another establishment to borrow some of the tools we needed for a job. They had all Caucasian workers with one African-American guy who Zach didn't know was my aunt's husband.

One day, my aunt's husband started telling me about all these rumors he heard about how I had performed all these sexual acts with Zach.

"They are all lies. I've never had sexual relations with Zach or any of my coworkers."

He was pissed off. He asked me if I wanted to have some guys catch him after work to straighten him out. I thought about it hard. I was crushed and disgusted.

He was always in my face pretending to be my friend. He would bring me food for lunch, which turned out to be a façade to make people think we were screwing around. I wish I would have known this a long time ago.

I knew how to play him after that. Never told him what I heard. I let him keep thinking he was getting away with his mission. Making himself look good while all along he was making me look like a tramp. I put it in God's hands. A couple months later, Zach hurt his back, eventually leaving on disability. Most of the people I started out working with were gone.

Harnes acted nice towards me, thinking that I didn't know his true intention. He thought it would lead to sex. I could see it in his eyes when he looked at me in that seductive way. I could hear it in his conversation with the cunning comments he made about me. I ignored it; I just kept doing my job.

Harnes had a worker from a different division come in to help him because he didn't know how to work the computer. Her name was Pam. When she first came around, I didn't say much to her since I didn't trust anyone I worked with. As time went on, she warmed up to me and we became pretty cool.

Rumors circulated about her and Harnes having an affair. I didn't think it was true at first until I kept catching them in compromising situations. I caught them in the office, in the park, plus their body language toward each other showed it. Here they are, both married and being unfaithful.

Pam and I grew closer. I would bring her tokens of appreciation to show her that I appreciated someone treating me fairly. I let her prepare my income taxes one year. When she got finished, she put the files on the lunchroom table. Everyone had left except me, her and Graham. I went to the ladies' room to freshen up. When I returned, my file was gone. I knew Graham took it, but I couldn't prove it. I told his boss about it the next day and they said there was nothing they could do because I had no proof. I was mad and there was nothing I could do about it.

Harnes started saying that we need to complete our CDL upgrade, but he didn't say why. He told a few other guys the reason, but none of the ladies or the African-American men. Harnes' friends that came from the other department already had a Class A CDL. We had no new equipment that required a Class A CDL so I didn't take it that seriously. I did the written part of the test, but I had not taken the road test.

Within a couple of months, some solid operator's positions became available. *This is the reasoning of the Class A license. He didn't say that.* I already knew how to operate the equipment required for the job. Some of the old-timers had shown me how to run it. I was getting paid out of class for running the equipment for my daily job assignments already. *I should be one of the people to get the position.* The guys Harnes brought in didn't know how to run it, I found out later he was sneaking them in after-hours training them to use the equipment. They already knew who they wanted to have the job and it wasn't me. I just needed to take the road test and I didn't think that would be a problem. We took the equipment operation test for the position and I aced the test; but to my surprise, a few weeks later, I got a letter saying I wasn't qualified for the job. Harnes' friends got the positions, none of the girls or minorities. I was so mad! I couldn't believe they screwed me out of the position without even trying to hide it, but they did. Harnes' friends were snickering. They knew if there was a layoff, they wouldn't be going. Though we had more seniority, their position was higher than ours.

Chapter 10

Not long after that, they came up with a new position and called it a conjoined worker. Conjoined workers were supposed to work in Harry's or Harnes' department, whichever one needed help that day. Harry finally got his foot in the door. I knew this couldn't be good. I didn't want any parts of it, but that's what they changed our title to.

After they forced these positions on us, Harnes called me in his office one day.

"You know you're about to get screwed, don't you?" Harnes asked.

"No, I'm not. The Lord is not going to let you do that to me."

"I don't know what kind of God you have." He started laughing.

As I was walking out of his office, I prayed, "Lord, I know you're not going to let them fire me for no good reason."

Days later, Reed and I were sent to Harry's department for what was supposed to be training. I walked in and all eyes were on me. I could feel cold, uncomfortable vibes in the air. The workers ran around like robots because Harry had them all afraid of him. He had another thing coming if he thought I would be acting like that.

Training was only going to be a week, so I decided to ignore him. He gave us our job assignment. I went out did it well. I was just shy of the so-called quota he said that other workers had to meet. He said it wasn't good enough. *My first day here and I'm just ten shy of the quota and that wasn't good enough? I thought it was darn good. Forget what he's talking about. I know I rocked it.*

The next couple of days were the same thing, barely under quota and him still complaining. *I can see where this is going; no matter what I do it won't be good enough to him.* Harry was supposed to be off work, but he rode down on me in his personal vehicle while I was out working, telling me I was walking too slowly. I didn't care. My knee was bothering me. I told him that and he laughed while pulling off. I had never done a job that required so much walking.

My knees starting swelling. I had injured them in the other department numerous times. I was so short, I had to basically jump into the trucks every time I got in them. The nurse at Chabo's clinic told them years prior that if they didn't put an extra step on the trucks so I could get in without jumping, it would give me knee problems. They didn't do what the nurse said. I began feeling the effects of knee trauma.

When Harry returned to work, I told him my knee was swollen from so much walking.

"What do you want me to do about it?" He asked. The union rep stood there and didn't say a word. I walked out and called Cody, the union president, to let him know what was going on. I told him my knees were swollen but tolerable, so I would try the job again. *This training session will be over soon, I can go back to my normal position in Harnes' department.*

The next morning when I got to work, Harry came running up to me yelling, "I don't know who you been talking to, but you and Reed are here to stay."

"That's not what the union president told me."

"We will see," he responded before storming off.

I called the union president and told him what happened. Cody said that's not part of the deal, that I was supposed to go back and forth between the two departments whoever needed me for that day or week.

When I got home that night after work, my knees were in pain and swelled more. I told Harry the next day about my knee again.

"You're lazy. You just don't want to do the job. Ain't nothing wrong with you. If it is, it isn't job-related," he said.

I was pissed. I told him I didn't have to lie about something being wrong with my knee, or about it being job-related. I've injured my knees plenty times in the other department.

He said, "Bull crap. Prove it."

When I got to work the next morning, I saw Reed and asked him to come in Harry's office with me as a witness in case he wouldn't send me to the clinic. To my surprise, he let me go. I went to the clinic and they said it was a chipped bone in my left knee from an old injury. They put me on limited duty until they got better; but said I couldn't do that job anymore. I took the clinic papers back to Harry, who started yelling and going ballistic.

"Well I don't know what you're going to do. If you can't do the jobs, quit!"

"I'm not quitting! I'm not going anywhere! Make me! I know other employees who had health issues and y'all accommodated them, so you're going to do the same for me or I'm calling the news or somebody!"

He looked at me with disgust. I didn't care. He knew I was right and I could prove it. He mumbled something and walked away.

The next morning Harry said he had nothing for me to do that fit the description of light duty, so he made me sit in the lunch room and read a book for the entire shift instead of letting me go home. The next day, he called me in the office and wrote me and Reed up for not meeting the quota on the job we were in training for. He dated it for the first day we started. *What? How do you get written up while in training on the first day?*

At that moment the Lord told me, "They're trying to give you a lot of write-ups to mess up your record, so they can fire you." *Thank you, Lord. This is the dirty game they are playing.* I called the union steward, told him I wanted to write a grievance protesting my write-up. One only had

72 hours to write a grievance before it's too late.

At the end of the shift, Harry was looking at me, rolling his eyes.

"I don't know who told you that you are only here for a week. You are here indefinitely. You're not going back to the other department," Harry said. We got into a full-blown argument.

"I'm not scared. You're not going to bully me."

The next day, I tried to contact the union steward. He wouldn't answer or return my phone calls. The union steward didn't want to write the grievance. I knew he didn't like me. He was one of the guys Harnes brought in and gave a higher position than me. He was mad because I made it known they screwed me out of that position. Plus, he feared Harry. He was always bragging about how nobody in his departments wrote grievances. *Well, your stats about to change because I'm writing one.*

I tried to get in touch with the union steward again to see what was taking so long to finish my grievance. He finally called back. He said he didn't write it.

I was mad and told him, "You'd better write it. If you're scared to do your job, resign."

He delayed it long as he could. He finally wrote it at the last minute because he knew I wasn't going to let it rest. I was happy I got the grievance in. They knew I wasn't playing games with them.

The atmosphere was tense; I was angry, and I didn't care. *I'm not about to sit here and let y'all screw me around. Y'all got me messed up.* My mind was going 100 miles a minute. *What can I do? I got to come up with another strategy.*

When I returned to work the next day, I was frustrated but couldn't let it show. I guess Harry was tired of me sitting at the table, so he put me on a different job that didn't require a lot of walking. We were cleaning out the sewers with this big truck. I was riding along helping the guy set up the equipment. When we were setting up my first day on the job, I looked down the street and there was a guy in a black Buick sitting there watching me. It looked like he was taking my picture. I didn't say anything to the guy I was with. I knew they were all on Harry's side if they wanted to be or not. They feared him. I ignored him and finished my job, although it made me very uncomfortable. It felt creepy to have a stranger standing by watching me. I knew Harry sent him. *What was his motive?*

It was finally time for the first step for the grievance I wrote. Harry told me it was at 2 o'clock.

"Make sure you are there on time," he said.

I'd been excited waiting for this meeting. *They knew they were wrong for writing us up. I know the union is going to put an end to this nonsense.*

I get in the meeting room and it was bright white with beautiful flowers.

The union steward looks at me and said, "You have no case. You got to take the write up."

I stood there speechless, trying to contemplate this bull crap he just said.

"What do you mean I have no case? Who gets wrote up in training?" *This can't be.*

I walked out and slammed the door so hard I tried to break it. The union said there was nothing they could do.

They aren't on our side. Chabo paid them not to help us a long time ago.

I sat there wondering who was going to help me. I'm not about to sit back and let them set me up to get fired. I called civil rights and told them what was going on. I made an appointment to go in. I took my write-ups with me, along with the union's response. They took my case.

When they contacted the job about my complaint, Harry was mad. He was yelling at everybody who came in his direction, I didn't care. Nobody was going to treat me like dirt and I just let them. I went down to civil rights after work and got all the paperwork together. I was so happy we were going to sue their behinds for doing me wrong. My case was strong. I received a call from civil rights a few days later. Chabo took the write up back so I no longer had a case. *What? You dirty bastards! I didn't have a write up in my file but that wasn't good enough there has got to be more I can do.*

Chapter 11

I had exhausted most of my resources. I was desperate. I was hurting. This was my last hope. I got the address to the homes of the executive board members, sent them a letter telling them everything these people had been doing to us girls plus the other minorities. I figured if I sent it to their home, they would read it and investigate what was going on without all the bosses knowing. The deception that ran throughout this company was deeper than I realized.

The next morning before getting to work, a coworker from Harnes' department called me.

"Did you write a letter to the executive board members?" He wanted to know.

"Yes, how did you know?

"Harnes has a copy of it. He's passing it out to everyone."

"What?"

"Yes, I thought I would warn you."

I was upset, but I didn't care, and I wasn't scared. I was fed up. I got to work, got my job assignment and went to work. While sitting there, I saw one of the superintendents pull up and hand Harry a piece of paper. It was the letter I wrote. They stood there for a while in a deep discussion. I tried to hear what they were saying. I couldn't figure it out.

I started strategizing what to do next. I had no help. I was in the battle alone. Afternoon break had finally arrived. I didn't want to be bothered with anybody. At the same time, I needed out of that garage. Upon entering the break room, I noticed everyone had a copy of the letter. There was a stack of them sitting on the break room table and they were posted all over the bulletin board. Everywhere.

I was distraught, but I couldn't let them see it. I collected my emotions, pretending it didn't faze me. They started making little remarks like, "Oh you wrote a letter to the board?" and "Were you talking about me on this part?"

I still didn't bend. They were trying to make me start acting like a fool so they could write me up. I refused to fall for it. I didn't care what they read or what they knew I did because even though they wouldn't admit it, they knew I was telling the truth. I decided to hold my head up, hold on to the truth, and continue to fight for my rights. *If I don't no one else will.*

A couple of days went by, and they were at it again. One of my extended family members wrote a poem for drama class. It was a great poem. She got an award for it. She gave me a copy; I put it on my locker. Two weeks later, Harry's assistant told me to go into the conference room.

"What for?"

"Just go. You'll find out when you get in there."

I got in there, one of the superintendents was already there; he was a black man, heavy set and light skinned.

"What's wrong? Do I need union representation?" He just stared at me like he didn't want to say whatever was on his mind. "What is it?"

I looked down and saw the poem from my locker on the table. *Didn't even notice it was missing off my locker.*

"The poem?"

He said, "Yes. People are complaining saying it could be racially offensive."

"All the racial bull crap that goes on around this place and y'all tripping about a poem? She wrote that in high school, won first place for it. The school didn't think it was racially offensive. Ok, this is a battle not worth fighting. I will take it down. All you had to do was ask. Holding a meeting trying to crucify me for it was unnecessary."

I walked outside looking at the rock piles, staring at the unclean environment surrounding me. Heaviness fell upon my mind. *I don't know what this is, but I don't like it.* I didn't know how much more of this I could take. I weighed my options. *Is the money even worth it anymore? Should I continue to put myself in this unhealthy situation?* I had invested too much of my time, 14 years had gone by. This was my livelihood. *Lord, help. I don't know what to do.*

After my knee swollen up, Harry continued sending me to the clinic every week for what he called a checkup. It was getting on my nerves. I didn't say anything. This went on for a while until one day the doctor asked me, "Why are you here again, Asia? What do they want?"

"They want you to say I can't work."

He said, "I'm not saying that. They better find something you can do."

They never sent me to the clinic for my knee anymore. Harry still wouldn't leave me alone. He saw me when I stopped to use the restroom and started yelling over the radio, "Come in the yard right now." When I got there, he told me to pull the weeds out of the fence line through the snow.

"I'm not doing it."

"Yes, you are!"

"No, I'm not. You will not degrade me just because I went to use the bathroom."

"Your kind isn't wanted here!"

"Well, my kind isn't going anywhere until I'm ready to leave."

"I'm writing you up if you don't pull those weeds out of the snow."

"I'm calling Arias at corporate." Arias said I didn't have to do it. Harry's face turned red, he ran off yelling. I chuckled inwards.

"Told you I wasn't doing that."

The next day he called a meeting saying if anybody wanted to use the restroom or anything they needed to get on the radio to get permission. After the meeting, I noticed everyone was still going to the restroom without asking permission. He wanted me to ask so he could keep up with me. The first couple of days I was able to hold out to use the restroom at break time.

One day, I couldn't hold it. I looked around the neighborhood, looking for a place I could safely use the restroom outside. I always carried tissue and water, so I could go plus wash my hands afterwards. The neighborhood was run down; a lot of houses were demolished, there were plenty of empty lots, nowhere private enough to hide. I decided to knock on somebody's door and ask if I could use the bathroom. That's what I did. I asked a total stranger if I could use the bathroom. She let me. My coworker couldn't believe I did that and he told Harry.

The weight of all the fighting was heavy on my mind. I started experiencing something I never experienced before, especially at this magnitude: Sadness. *What is wrong? Why can't I shake this feeling?* I felt lost, alone, defeated. I didn't know what to do. Suddenly, tears started flowing. They wouldn't stop. I cried all day and all night. *What is wrong with me? I'm a strong woman. I don't cry. What is this? I don't like it. Something is wrong. I'm going to the hospital.*

I went to get some medical attention. The doctor asked me what was going on in my life. Who's getting on your nerves? What is it? I told him I do nothing but work and go home. I explained to him all the chaos, fussing and fighting I was dealing with on the job. While the hurt from my heart kept flowing in the form of tears, he looked at me with compassion and care. He was heaven sent.

"The people on the job are a big part of your problem. That is not a healthy environment for you. It's been too much for too long now. It is affecting you. You are experiencing what is called depression. I'm taking you off work until next week. Go see your doctor and tell him what is going on."

I left and went to see my own doctor. My doctor had medical issues going on. He wasn't practicing medicine at that moment. *Lord, what am I going to do? I have no doctor. No other doctor will understand me. I need You to help lead me to the right doctor who's going to take care of me. I have nowhere to turn.* I had no more fight left in me. They broke me down. No money, no man, no nothing was worth me losing my happiness for. I stayed home the next few days crying, upset, feeling the lowest I had ever felt. Just thinking that I had to go back and deal with those people next week wasn't helping; it made me feel hopeless. *Lord, give me strength.*

While at home trying to deal with my issues, I looked out of my kitchen window which was adjacent to a country club that had a huge parking lot. Harnes was sitting there in his truck parked toward my kitchen window, trying to look through my window with what looked like binoculars. *Why won't they just back off and leave me alone?* A few hours later, I was sitting on the couch looking out of the window, trying to put my emotions back in order and here comes Harry. *This is not cool. I'm not at work and they were still harassing me. I'm going to ignore them before I get angry and run outside and have it out with them. I'm sick of them.*

The next week I found a clinic to go to that kept me off work for a few more weeks. I was glad. I needed a break and I needed to figure out what I was going to do next. While I was off, I started getting my resume together. *I need to find another job. I got to get away from these prejudiced people. They are crazy.* The time went fast. It was time to go back to the war zone. Oh, how I dreaded that day. I got to deal with it a little while longer until I find a new job.

Chapter 12

I got to work that day and the clique was laughing. *I don't care. Nobody better not run up in my face saying nothing unless they're ready to be slapped because that's exactly what I'm going to do. Since they think I'm a joke, I'm gonna give them something to laugh about.* I got my job assignment and went on about my business. Harry didn't come into the break room. I didn't see him that day which was pleasant for me. *Wish I never had to see him again in my life.* The end of the shift didn't come fast enough for me then it was finally over.

I went into the restroom to freshen up like I usually do. *Thank God. Let me out of this place.* I was surprised at how quiet the day was. I went home, took a bath and broke out in tears again. I thought this was over, but I guess it wasn't. I gathered myself, smoked a blunt, trying to calm my mind. Went into my bedroom, closed myself off from everybody and enjoyed the peace of my own world for those few hours before falling asleep.

As soon as I got to work the next day, one of my coworkers came rushing up to me saying, "Come with me. I have to show you something, but you have to promise you won't say anything. Please don't tell them I told you or I will receive backlash." I told her I wouldn't say anything.

Upon entering the room, she had a counter-letter that Harry had his clique write. My very own union brothers were saying I was a disgruntled worker who just didn't want to do her job because they changed the division I worked in. I guess they prepared it to give to the board members.

When I read it, I wasn't shocked. I didn't expect anything less coming from this secret society that they engaged in. As I went out to get my job assignment, they called me in the office and presented me with the letter. The agitated look in their eyes told me that they were waiting for me to explode like I usually would've done. They didn't know I already knew about it.

My fight was leaving me. I had no more fight left. I was bruised, tired, and ready to quit this job. I had enough. They were killing me inside. *Y'all are the ones harassing me, giving me a hard time. Just because I fight for my rights, I'm disgruntled.* Make this make sense to me.

I took the letter, said, "Oh well" and walked out of the

office. The look of disappointment fell upon their faces while inside I was laughing because they didn't get the pleasure they were looking for from me.

I went on doing my job but only the bare minimum because nothing I did would ever please them. I decided I wasn't going above and beyond for them anymore. That was over. They knew I was still smoking marijuana. It was killing them that they couldn't prove it. So, they broke all kinds of rules trying to prove it; but their tactics failed.

I prepared to go home for the day. I went into the ladies' locker room to freshen up. I left my duffel bag by the floor because there wasn't anything valuable in it. I reached to get my hairbrush; it was gone. *This doesn't make sense. I'm tired of them stealing my things.*

I asked the female coworkers, "Have y'all seen my brush? A couple said no, but another one said she saw it on top of my bag earlier that day. *Somebody was in my bag messing with my things because the bag was zipped up when I left it earlier.*

I called Arias and told him what was going on. He was

mad as well as I was. *This don't make no sense. They're stealing my gloves, my glasses, and any other item they can just to get on my nerves.* He told me to call the police the next time anything of mine came up missing; he was tired of the foolishness. Right after I hung up with him, a coworker came into the bathroom. I told her what was going on. She said she overheard them saying they took my hairbrush, so they can take the hair out of it to drug test it. *What? That is illegal.*

I called the union president and told him what my coworker told me.

He said, "Don't worry about it. If they say anything about any drugs or anything else they found in your system through your hair that they stole, this thing will blow up majorly. You will have a law suit. It is illegal. They will have to admit to stealing your item and illegally drug testing your hair. Do what Arias said. Call the police."

If looks could kill, I would be dead. Harry was annoyed. I was laughing because the weekend before, I was hanging out with some of the fellas. We had smoked major blunts. I even drank some syrup mixed with pop. He went looking, he found it, and there was nothing he could do about it. From that day forth, none of my things came up missing again.

Harry wasn't giving up that easy. He had another trick up his sleeve that manifested a couple of weeks later. When I was off work, I noticed the guy in that black Dodge that was watching me before riding by my house. *Who is this guy and what does he want with me? This is creepy. He is stalking me in a sense. I got to find out who he is.*

I caught him riding by my house and got the license plate number. A friend of mine ran the license plate. I was totally shocked when I got the results back. He said it was a government car being used by the police who were watching gangs. *What? Why would the police be watching me?*

He said, "Didn't you know Harry is the union steward for the police department?"

I didn't know but it made a whole lot of sense. Harry was trying to get his cop friends to bust me for marijuana. *This is wrong on so many levels, you prejudiced cocaine-*

snorting alcoholic, trying to mess me all the way up when you're doing more wrong than me. Got your police buddy in on it, too. Now that I know what's going on, I must strategically watch my steps. This is serious; he's trying to get me put in jail. This guy is way eviler than I imagined. I have never been to jail and I'm not planning on going any time soon. I'm not going to say anything. I'm going to pretend like I don't know.

Chapter 13

The meddling and arguments never ceased, ultimately sending me spiraling into depression again. This was too much for me to handle on my own. I needed to talk to someone. I found a counselor through job services who everyone warned me not to go to because they worked for the company. But come to find out, they were wrong. They were good counselors who truly cared about their patients.

She wasn't even surprised as I started telling her about my experiences. She had other clients who worked for Chabo and dealt with some of the same things I was going through. She connected me with the doctor who worked in the same building, so they could communicate with each other about me. She made me an appointment to go see him.

By the time my appointment came with him a month later, I was so mentally damaged I could barely think. This thing called depression had robbed me of my life. The weight of all the chaos had dragged me down to a place I had never been before. The heaviness that captured my heart, these tear drops of blood pouring out of my soul, was too much to bear. I was broken. They had made an impact upon my life that wasn't going away.

The doctor said, "This is enough. I am not sending you back there. I am taking you off indefinitely."

I should have felt some relief after hearing those words, but I didn't. The damage had been done and I didn't know if I would ever be the same happy, spirited, full of life person I used to be. I didn't even know how to get back there. *Lord, have mercy on me.*

I got all the paper work needed from the doctor to take to the job. I went through the front and dropped it off with the secretary, not even thinking about seeing management. I didn't want to see them or talk to them anyway.

I got home, and the tears wouldn't stop. Day and night, they were flowing. I couldn't eat. I couldn't sleep. I couldn't think. I just stayed in the bed or on the couch. I slept or cried all day. When I looked out the window every day they were right there. I mean every department all day long up and down my block. *This is so pathetic.* My mother called me. They were riding by her house and my sister's house also. *What is wrong with these people? They are sick and about to make me snap.*

I got fed up and called the union president. I told him this needed to stop. They were trying to get me to start a fight with one of them, so they could press charges on me or something. They had no clue how hard dealing with depression was. I couldn't go there with them. I'm scared of what I might do to one of them. He asked me if I would go in front of the board members to submit my complaint although they were the ones that were supposed to have kept my letter private. We would be in front of other citizens, plus it's televised. I said yes. I prepared myself throughout the week trying to figure out exactly what I was going to say.

The next week it was time for me to go. I was scared. I was nervous. But I wasn't going to let them see it in me. When I sat there waiting for my turn to speak, I got hard, cold stares. *I don't care. I'm going to say what I need to say whether they wanted to hear it or not.*

The union president had schooled me on how to stand, how to say and do what I needed to do.

I asked them to please tell Harry, the rest of the foremen, and that police guy to please leave me and my family alone or I'm going to take legal action. They looked as if they didn't have a clue what I was talking about but said they would investigate.

I didn't feel like I made any progress, but I was happy I stood up for me. I stood up for what was right. I hoped what I said helped someone else from going through the same thing.

The harassment slowed up, but it didn't stop completely. Although I never saw the black Dodge again, I knew I would never have peace living in their jurisdiction. I gave my house back and moved. Finally, I received a little peace. I can look out of my window and not see Chabo's trucks riding by or parked around my house watching and waiting for whatever.

As I progress forward, toward getting back to a sense of normalcy, the heaviness that weighs upon my mind has barely lifted. I realize this is something that is not going away easily or any time soon. I will continue pressing

forward, even with tear drops of blood dripping down my face.

Enjoy these poems

by

Marlo Donald

from

Crying From the Pain

Available on

www.MarloDonald.com

And wherever books are sold

Tear Drops of Blood: The Poem

Red drops pouring out of my soul...

Falling out of my eye ducts...

They have taken control.

Running like water... out of a faucet.

Got me feeling defeated... laying in my prayer closet.

Just like fire shut up in my bones...

Got my mind running rampant in an offensive zone.

Tear drops of blood rolling down my face.

Feel like coals on a fire...

Burning in one place.

Mind stuck on replay…

Experiencing the same thoughts over and over again.

Make you think you're alone…

With not one single friend.

Even with the tears flowing and flowing.

I got to keep pressing… Keep going and going.

I pray they stop one day… I pray they stop soon.

Morning… Evening… Day or night…

I don't care if it's noon.

Lord, unbreak my heart so my soul will stop bleeding.

Fill it with love and kindness… Give me a new reason.

Let me dwell in your secret place…

To begin my healing season.

Dry up these teardrops of blood…

That came in like a flood.

I know you are my refuge…

My safety place.

And I will always trust you…

No matter what others say.

Blood stains no trace…With a smile… you will replace.

INJUSTICE INJUSTICE

Injustice ... Injustice

Why am I dealing with you?

Is it the color of my skin? or to my race I am true.

Injustice... Injustice.

I did nothing to meet you face to face.

But here I am starring at you feeling this disgrace.

Injustice ... Injustice.

I don't like how you make me feel.

Unwanted...Incomplete... and think I'm ready to steal.

You think I'm trying to rob you... But you're robbing me.

Taking my freedom to feel safe... My freedom to be free.

Minorities getting killed for no rhyme or reason.

You wearing the badge of honor.

But think it's purging season.

You have no right to take an innocent life.

Got the nation in an uproar turning blacks against whites.

You are the ones that supposed to keep this land together.

But you're breaking it into pieces.

Like rain drops in bad weather.

Injustice... Injustice

Your making people not know what to do.

So they are reacting with violence.

Because… they are tired of you.

Injustice… Injustice

Will you ever treat people fair?

I don't think you will.

Because… you don't even care.

As Long as He's With You

Worship God with all your might

So you can make it through this life.

With faith and peace underneath your feet...

That stand on solid ground

Even if man puts you down.

God will hold on strong will never let you go.

Keep you grounded... Keep you safe...

Over your face... Over your life...

While fighting those perilous fights of life.

Just as long as He's with you...

You will stand tall through the storms and the rain.

Just as long as He's with you….

You will hold up strong…

Even while walking through pain.